ELIZABETH COLE

MY WAY TO GOOD CHOICES

ILLUSTRATED BY
TATYANA KIM

Book by Elizabeth Cole

This book belongs to

....

....

Melissa likes to spend time playing on the playground.
She likes to help others and spread kindness all around.
But when she has to make a choice, she may not do it right,
and the result is her behavior becomes rude and impolite.

One day, Melissa was shopping with her mom at the mall,
but couldn't wait to get home to play with her new doll.
She showed it to her brother, and in one fell swoop,
he grabbed Melissa's doll and dipped it in his soup.

Melissa widened her eyes and her cheeks turned red.
A volcano of anger was about to erupt in her head.
She started to shout, but that wasn't enough for her to do;
she took her baby brother's favorite toy and broke it in two.

Melissa started to sulk, but the baby pouted more as he stared at his fire truck lying on the floor. While her baby brother cried all the tears he had, little Melissa began to feel very upset and sad.

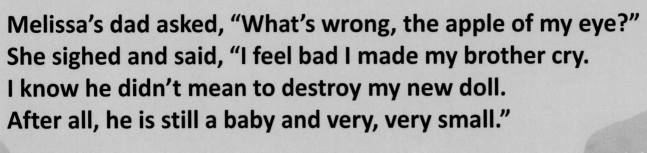

Melissa's dad asked, "What's wrong, the apple of my eye?"
She sighed and said, "I feel bad I made my brother cry.
I know he didn't mean to destroy my new doll.
After all, he is still a baby and very, very small."

Melissa's dad smiled softly and stroked her worried head.
"Each of our actions has consequences," he gently said.
"Nothing good comes out of yelling and raising your voice.
What kind of day you will have depends on your choice.

Here are some tips to stop your sudden reaction.
Always think twice before you take any action.
When you feel angry, imagine smelling a rose.
Close your eyes and inhale through the nose.

Watch as your belly rises up like a balloon.
Don't let the air out of your lungs too soon.
After two seconds, slowly blow the air out.
It will help you feel better, without a doubt.

Think about the consequences after you calm down.

Will your choice bring you
a smile or a frown?

How will your decision
affect those around you?

If you think carefully,
you'll know what to do."

Melissa decided to follow her dad's wise advice.
Before any action, she would always think twice.
The next day, when her mom told her to make the bed,
Melissa wanted to say "No!" but thought well instead.

She thought about it. My mom is always there for me.
She is caring and loving and fills my days with glee.
If I ignore Mom's words, it might hurt her feelings, too.
I don't like making the bed, but it's the least I can do.

Melissa smiled cheerfully and began to tidy up her room.
She first made her bed, and then she reached for a broom.
When she was done, Melissa said, "Mom, close your eyes!"
Her mom stood in the doorway, stunned by the nice surprise.

The next day, Melissa and her family visited the zoo.
There, she wanted so badly to feed the kangaroo.
But the sign said *No!*, which made Melissa feel sad.
Then she recalled the advice spoken by her dad.

I could feed the kangaroo behind the guard's back.
I could give him some ice cream, my favorite snack.
But then the animal might get a tummy ache.
That would be awful, and a huge mistake.

"I will follow all the zoo rules," little Melissa said.
She looked around and found the zookeeper instead.
Together, they fed kangaroos what they usually eat.
The little joey was so happy, so cuddly and sweet.

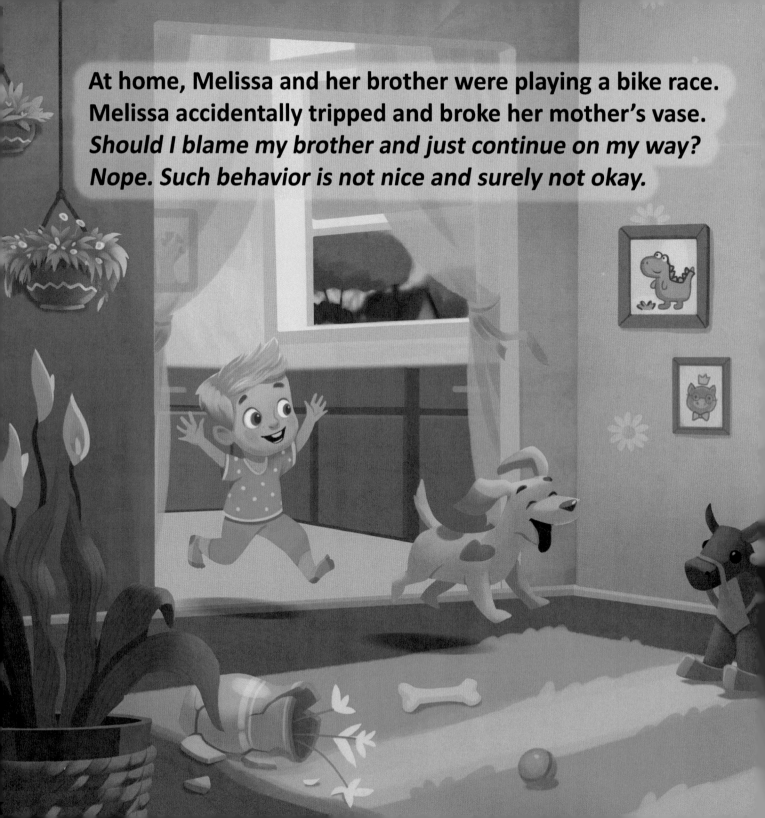

At home, Melissa and her brother were playing a bike race.
Melissa accidentally tripped and broke her mother's vase.
Should I blame my brother and just continue on my way?
Nope. Such behavior is not nice and surely not okay.

Melissa decided it was important to be honest and fair.
"It was me. I'm sorry," she admitted, showing that she cared.
"I promise I'll buy you a new vase with my pocket money."
Her mother smiled and said, "I'm so proud of you, honey."

At school, during math class, Melissa had a lot to say.
She didn't interrupt the teacher, but thought this way:
What if everyone spoke at once with a loud voice?
No one would hear anyone's words with all that noise.

So, Melissa waited to speak until the teacher was done.
The other kids saw this and raised their hands one by one.
The teacher praised them all for being patient and polite,
and each got a *Good Behavior* badge so shiny and bright.

On the playground, Melissa was having fun and feeling joy,
when her friend Sam came and asked to borrow her toy.
Melissa paused and thought about what she should do.
Sharing is an act of kindness and true friendship, too.

If I say, *No! That's mine!* my friend Sam could get sad.
So, little Melissa considered all the choices she had.
I choose not to be selfish, but show how much I care.
I always want to be a good friend, so I choose to share.

Melissa tries to make good choices every single day.
But sometimes she makes mistakes, and that's okay.
Next time, I'll do better, and I'll behave right.
I choose to make all my days happy and bright.

I CAN CHOOSE

MAKE A MESS IN YOUR ROOM

HAVE TO STAY AND
CLEAN IT UP

KEEP YOUR ROOM TIDY

GO TO PLAY WITH YOUR
FRIENDS AND HAVE FUN

**TELL A LIE ABOUT HELPING
YOUR GRANNY**

PARENTS ARE UPSET AND
MIGHT NOT BELIEVE YOU

HELP YOUR GRANNY

PARENTS ARE PROUD
OF YOU AND GRANNY WILL
COOK YOUR FAVORITE CAKE

**MAKE FUN OF SOMEBODY
WHO FELL INTO A PUDDLE**

OTHERS THINK THAT YOU
ARE MEAN

GIVE A HELPING HAND

YOU CAN MAKE A NEW FRIEND

GO TO BED TOO LATE

FEEL TIRED THE NEXT DAY
AND GET A BAD GRADE

GO TO SLEEP ON TIME

FEEL FULL OF ENERGY
AND WIN THE DEBATES
COMPETITION

EAT TOO MUCH CANDY

HAVE A TUMMY ACHE

EAT HEALTHY FOOD

FEEL GREAT AND STAY
STRONG

Dear little reader,

Have you ever faced a tough choice and wondered if you made the right decision? Well, you're not alone!
Just like Melissa, we all have moments when we're not sure what to do. I hope that with the guidance this book
offers you've discovered the importance of consequences and learnt to think twice before taking any action.

I'm thrilled to share Melissa's journey with you, and I hope it has inspired you
to make good choices in your own life. Your thoughts and feedback mean the world to me,
and they'll help me create more exciting stories in this series. Yes, you read that right –
there are more adventures with Melissa to come! Can you imagine what challenges
she might face next time? Share your ideas with me, and you might see them come to life
in one of the upcoming books. How exciting would that be?

Thank you for joining me on this incredible journey of discovery and growth.
I can't wait to hear from you! You can write to me at
elizabethcole.author@gmail.com or visit www.ecole-author.com.
Your input means a lot to me!

You can leave your review of this book here:

With love,
Elizabeth Cole

GO HERE
TO GET YOUR
COLORING PAGE

Made in the USA
Las Vegas, NV
05 May 2024

89549908R00019